FLORIDA SANTA

Is He Real?
How Do We Know It?

Santa is real!
EnJOY
Ruth E. Clark

Ruth E. Clark

Illustrations by
Sarah Caterisano

HIBISCUS PUBLISHING
About Books for Children

First Edition. Second Printing

Library of Congress Cataloging-in-Publication Data

Clark, Ruth E.
Florida Santa—Is He Real? How Do We Know It? : two children visit grandparents in
    Florida where Christmas traditions are quite different raising many questions and
    concerns in their preparations for Florida Santa's expected deliveries / Ruth E. Clark

  ISBN-13: 978-0-9792963-0-7
  ISBN-10: 0-9792963-0-7

  [1. Santa – Fiction. 2. Florida – Fiction. 3. Christmas – Fiction.] I. Title

                                                                      2007922576

Printed in the USA

For Amelia and Matthew

"I will honor Christmas in my heart,
And try to keep it all year . . . "
<small>CHARLES DICKENS</small>

Soon it will be Christmas.
Amelia and I can't wait.
We're going to Florida,
The Sunshine state.

We're so excited.
Can you guess the reason?
We're visiting Grandma and Grandpa
This happy season.

love, Grandma & Grandpa

Images of Christmas
     are all around—
Light, candles, and snow;
Gingerbread cookies
     and candy canes—
We're getting ready to go.

Our luggage is packed:
Toothbrushes,
PJs, and
Slippers.

And don't forget . . .
Bathing suits,
Goggles, and
Flippers.

Amelia packed
Her special red dress.
Sisters and Grandmas
Like that I guess.

I packed
Old jeans and a tee.
Fishing is fun
For Grandpa and me.

A Florida Christmas is different
It seems to me.

Let's get ready—
Shopping, Wrapping, and
Cutting down a tree.

There are so many questions
And things to prepare.
If we go to Florida,
Will Santa find us there?

What about our letters
Which we mailed in CA?
Will Santa look for us at home,
Or remember we're away?

Here in Florida
If there's no snow,
How will Santa's sleigh
Come and go?

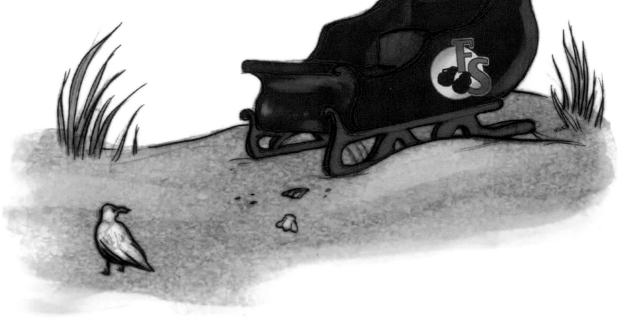

I have questions about chimneys and
How Santa comes with a bound.
I have looked and looked,
No chimney can be found.

With his fur-trimmed boots
And long beard of white,
Won't Santa be too warm
This before Christmas night?

I know that my home
Is really far away.
How can Santa get everywhere
On the very same day?

Is there one Santa or many?
How can we know?
How can he get here
If it doesn't snow?

Christmas in Florida
Seems so very confusing.
If Santa doesn't find me,
It won't be amusing.

Grandma says, "A sleigh and reindeer
Are not appropriate here.
Florida Santa and his helpers
Need trucks they can steer."

Grandma says all of this
Shouldn't worry me.
Florida Santa may come by boat
Or in a roomy SUV.

"Santa has a plan," Grandma says.
"He checks lists and reports.
Florida Santa and his helpers
Wear flip-flops and shorts."

Grandma answers my questions
With confidence and ease.
I understand the messages,
But PLEASE, PLEASE, PLEASE.

My head is whirling
With questions and thoughts;
Especially those important
SHOULD I(s) and OUGHTS.

Since I arrived in Florida
Just two days ago,
Ought I remind Santa
Or will he already know?

Should I write Santa another note?
What ought I say?
"I'm here in Florida.
Please find me Christmas day."

Should I hang up my stocking?
Where ought it be?
On the lanai, by the pool,
Or under the tree?

Should I leave cookies and milk
As is custom it would seem?
Ought it be key lime pie
And lots of whipped cream?

Oh dear me, my poor little head.
I try to understand what Grandma has said.
There is one question I have yet to ask.
The biggest question, so I've saved it for last.

When I ask Grandma she gives answers
She says she's found to be true.
And so I'll ask Grandma the B I G G I E,
What else can I do?

Is Santa Real?
How Do I Know It?
I need to be sure.
I don't want to blow it.

All I need to know about Santa,
Grandma says, she'll tell me again.
Things which have been true
Since she can't remember when.

Grandma says chimneys and snow all around
Are not important for children to be found.
We need to spread much love and care
To assure each child that Santa will be there.

All through the year
We must be kind to others.
To grown ups and friends,
To our sisters and brothers.

Our caring and love
Must fill the air.
Grandma knows that love
Finds children everywhere.

As Santa in his North Pole home
Prepares for this special season,
He is also filled with love;
And so has good reason

To fill up his sack
Year after year.
Children can be sure
He soon will be here.

Our PJs are on.
Our teeth are brushed and clean.
Our stockings are hung
Where they can be seen.

We've left cookies and milk.
We've signed our notes too.
We must be ready.
What else can we do?

Grandma assures me that all will be well.
When Santa looks around he can tell
That Amelia and I are tucked in our beds
with happy thoughts filling our heads.

This Christmas Eve
As we climb into bed,
We think a lot
About all Grandma said.

Christmas morning, as the room fills
with light,
We awaken from what seems a very
long night.
I look at Amelia and Amelia looks at me.
Did we hear something? What could
it be?

IT WAS! HE DID!
    GRANDMA WAS RIGHT!
Santa did find us this
    Christmas night.

The toys have arrived
And even a letter.
All things considered,
It makes me feel better.

"Dear Amelia and Matt"
Is what Santa wrote.
"Have a Happy Christmas
And thanks for your note."

Dear Amelia & Matt,
Have a Happy Christmas.
Thanks for your note.

Florida Santa

I pondered and thought.
How could this be?
Guess what Florida Santa
Left for Amelia and me?

It wasn't skates,
And no, not a sled.
Florida Santa brought us
Skimmer boards instead.

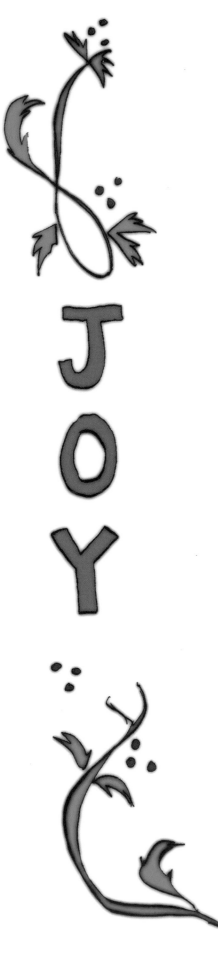

Is Santa real?
How do we know it?
These questions seem to remain.
One more time Grandma says she
    will explain.

"So many questions, dear children,
On matters great and small.
I want to be sure
To answer them all."

"Santa," said Grandma, "is not
Just a guy who brings toys.
The spirit of Santa is giving—
The true Christmas JOY."

"Santa reminds us
To make children happy
So they learn love
And not fear.
        That's the reason
            Santa comes
            Year after year."

"To keep Santa real," Grandma explains,
"We must all do our part.
The spirit of Santa must spread
Through love given heart to heart."

"Amelia and Matt,
And children who love and care,
All help keep Santa real
In Florida and everywhere."

"People agree," Grandma says, "that
Santa comes in December.
But we need Santa's spirit all year
When it's hard to remember."

"We should share Santa's spirit
In February, March, and July.
You know Santa is REAL,
And now you know why."

Oh yes, SANTA IS REAL!
I'm sure and I know it.
I'll take Grandma's advice
And spread love to show it.

The End

Acknowledgments

To my husband and life partner, Carl, who gives generously of
his encouragement and faith in me.

To son, Brian, and daughter-in-law, Diane, who have given
the gifts of love and guidance to our grandchildren.

To Amelia Sophie and Matthew Aaron who continuously
shine giving unspoken assurances of Spirit's grace
and abundant love.

To children everywhere—may they learn love; and through
giving love, spread the spirit of Santa and the
true Christmas Joy.

A special thank you to friends for encouraging a grandmother
to go for dreams long delayed by life's toils and distractions.

About the Author

Dr. Ruth E. Clark is a retired educator having worked with children and families for more than thirty years in public and private schools in New Jersey. She holds an earned doctorate from Temple University, Philadelphia.

Dr. Clark resides in Naples, Florida.

About the Illustrator

Sarah Caterisano attends The Ringling School of Art and Design in Sarasota, Florida where she is an Illustration major.

Florida Santa is Sarah's second published children's book. Sarah plans to practice as a freelance illustrator. Her goal is to teach children and adults in her own studio.

Sarah is from Allen, Texas.

About Hibiscus Publishing

Hibiscus Publishing is **A**bout **B**ooks for **C**hildren and based upon the philosophy that the lives of all children are enriched through exposure and experiences with the written word. There is no farther-reaching endeavor than to read to a child; thereby opening the mind to exciting explorations of reality and dreams.

Read to Someone You Love

HIBISCUS PUBLISHING

About Books for Children

HIBISCUS PUBLISHING
About Books for Children

Coming from Hibiscus Publishing in 2008

Whilomeena . . . Loves White

Airport Mouse

Airport Mouse Works The Night Shift

Airport Mouse Explores On Opening Day

Airport Mouse Becomes A VIP/VIM World Traveler

Look for these titles in your favorite bookstore mid-2008
or contact Hibiscus Publishing at:
hibiscus311@comcast.net